W9-ATY-643

DISCARD

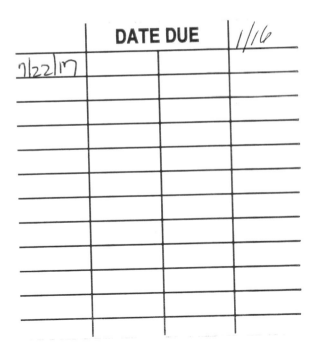

VOLLEYBALL VICTORY

BY JAKE MADDOX

text by Leigh McDonald
illustrated by Katie Wood

STONE ARCH BOOKS
a capstone imprint

Jake Maddox Girl Sports Stories are published by Stone Arch Books
a Capstone imprint
1710 Roe Crest Drive
North Mankato, Minnesota 56003
www.mycapstone.com

Library of Congress Cataloging-in-Publication Data

Maddox, Jake, author.
Volleyball victory / by Jake Maddox ; text by Leigh McDonald ; illustrated
by Katie Wood.
pages cm. -- (Jake Maddox girl sports stories)

Summary: Andrea is looking forward to another winning volleyball season
with her school team, but the new coach is putting them through a lot of
basic drills, and Andrea is frustrated because she is not playing the position
she is used to, and she does not understand why.

ISBN 978-1-4965-2619-9 (library binding) -- ISBN 978-1-4965-2621-2 (pbk.) --
ISBN 978-1-4965-2623-6 (ebook pdf)

1. Volleyball--Juvenile fiction. 2. Teamwork (Sports)--Juvenile fiction.
3. Frustration--Juvenile fiction. [1. Volleyball--Fiction. 2. Teamwork
(Sports)--Fiction.] I. McDonald, Leigh, 1979- author. II. Wood, Katie, 1981-
illustrator. III. Title.

PZ7.M25643Vr 2016
813.6--dc23
[Fic]
2015024020

Designer: Kristi Carlson
Production Specialist: Lori Barbeau

Artistic Elements: Shutterstock

Printed in the United States of America in Stevens Point, Wisconsin.
092015   009222WZS16

TABLE OF CONTENTS

Chapter One

TALKING ABOUT TRYOUTS

It was hot. Too hot to move. Summer was almost over, and Andrea couldn't wait for fall to begin. Boot weather! Apple cider! Volleyball!

At the thought of volleyball, Andrea sat up quickly. Just last night, her mom had told her that the coach she'd had for the past three years was moving to California. Coach Warren had been great — she'd led the team to many victories. How would this year go with a new coach?

Maybe Rose, her best friend and teammate, had heard more about it. Andrea raced to her computer, brought up chat, and began typing.

> **Andrea:** *Did you hear about Coach Warren leaving? Crazy!*

> **Rose:** *Yes! So sad. :(*

> **Andrea:** *I know, she was my fave! Any idea who might coach this year?*

> **Rose:** *No. But I guess we find out next week at tryouts!*

> **Andrea:** *YAY! Ugh, it is seriously TOO HOT. Want to go swimming?*

> **Rose:** *Yes, please! See you at the pool in half an hour?*

> **Andrea:** *Sounds great!*

Andrea dashed to get her bathing suit on. Relief from the heat at last!

When she arrived at the pool, Andrea saw Rose already in the water talking to a girl she didn't recognize. Andrea ditched her bag and shorts by a lounge chair and jumped into the pool. She splashed up from her dunk with a happy sigh and swam over to her friend.

"Hey!" Andrea called out to the two girls.

"Hi, Andrea!" Rose said. "This is Zoe. She moved to my street a couple of weeks ago."

The girl in the lace-patterned bathing suit smiled. "Nice to meet you," Zoe said.

"I was just telling her that she should join the volleyball club this fall," said Rose. She turned back to Zoe, paddling easily. "Andrea is an awesome setter. It's a super fun team — we're called the Pumas. We even won Regionals last year!"

"I don't know. I haven't really played volleyball before," Zoe said uncertainly. "It does sound like fun, though."

"You should totally try out," Andrea urged. "Why not? It's such a blast."

Zoe smiled. "I'll think about it!" she said.

Just then, the girls were startled by a huge splash as some boys jumped into the deep end. They shrieked and slapped water back at the boys, starting a water fight that was quickly ended by the lifeguard's whistle.

Rose laughed as the three girls swam away. "If we can be such a good team in the pool," she began, "imagine how great we'll be on the volleyball court!"

Andrea put her arms around Zoe and Rose. "For sure!" Andrea said. "Even without Coach Warren, this will be the best season ever!"

Chapter Two

THE NEW COACH

The following week, the rec center gym echoed with excited chatter. The room was packed with girls ready for volleyball tryouts. As soon as Andrea walked through the double doors, her friends surrounded her.

"Andrea! You're here!" Hannah cried, hugging her.

"Are you ready?" Rose asked. "I can't wait. I've been practicing with Zoe all weekend."

"Oh, she's coming? Awesome!" Andrea said. She looked around the busy gym. "Have you met the new coach yet?"

"No," Emily said, joining the group, "but she has to be here somewhere. Let's look around."

They didn't need to look for very long — just then, a shrill whistle pierced the air. All conversations came to a quick stop, and everyone turned to see a small, kind-looking man in a blue tracksuit holding a clipboard.

"Hello, new and returning players! Welcome to the Junior Club Volleyball tryouts," the man said. "My name is Coach Tucker. I'm your new coach this year, and I'm really looking forward to getting to know you all. Now, let's group up by the first court."

Once all the girls had gathered together, the coach gave them a big smile. "I first want to say how excited I am to be here," he said. "If you work hard, I promise you'll have fun and learn a lot. If we win some matches, too, that will just be an added bonus."

Andrea frowned a little. She liked having fun, but she also liked winning.

Coach Tucker continued: "I want to begin by looking at your passing skills. Can the girls from last year's team please raise their hands?"

Andrea's hand shot into the air, along with several others.

"Great," Coach said. He pointed at Andrea and Meg. "Can you two please demonstrate passing?" He tossed the ball to Meg, who trotted off to the opposite side of the court.

Andrea got into position with her hands together and arms straight out in front of her. She bent low at the waist and knees.

Meg tossed the ball over the net. Andrea easily hit it back over to her teammate.

"Perfect," the coach said. "See her straight arms? Knowing the basics is key to becoming a great volleyball player. I want you all to pair up and practice the pass."

The girls began pairing off and passing the balls back and forth over the net. The coach moved off to the side and made some notes on his clipboard.

Andrea walked over to Rose, and they exchanged a look. This new coach seemed so much more laid back than their old coach. He wasn't at all what they had expected. What would the Pumas be like this year?

Chapter Three

BACK TO BASICS

Fweet! The coach's whistle echoed through the gym, followed by the thump of volleyballs hitting the floor. Coach Tucker jogged over to have a word with Zoe. She was working on her setter skills and was having some trouble controlling the ball.

Andrea sighed. She was annoyed. Last year, she had played setter and loved it. This year, she'd barely had a chance to show the new coach her setting skills.

It was already the second week of team practice, and Coach Tucker was still spending practices rotating the girls through all the positions. He said that it would make them "well-rounded" and that it would give him a chance to find the best position for each girl.

But Andrea knew what she was best at — being a setter. *It's definitely not Zoe, that's for sure*, she thought. *How are we ever going to win if our setter can't even set?*

Coach Tucker blew his whistle again. "Everyone, hustle in!" he hollered. "We're going to watch a little video."

The team gathered by the net, where the coach had his laptop set up on a chair. Andrea made her way over more slowly than the rest of the girls.

"This is a video of the practice game we ran the other day," Coach said as he hit *play*. "I want you to pay attention to what you all do with your arms whenever the ball is hit."

The girls watched themselves hit the ball back and forth over the net. Each time someone bumped the volleyball, the rest of the players brought their arms together in order to be ready to hit it back.

Andrea shrugged. *What's wrong with that?*

"See how you all bring your arms together in front of your body before you even know where the ball is headed?" the coach asked. "That's wasted motion. Unless it lands in front of you, you'll have to swing your whole body and both arms over to meet it. I want you to try this."

Coach motioned to Emily. "Emily, please toss a ball to me, just a little off to one side." While Emily went to grab a ball, Coach took up a position. He bent his knees and held both of his arms out to the sides. It looked very weird.

But when Emily tossed the ball, he swung his right arm over to meet his left. He hit the volleyball and sent it straight back to Emily. Coach Tucker had barely moved at all. He stood up and smiled.

"Do you see the difference? There's less movement," Coach explained. "Please pair up and give it a try."

Andrea blew out an annoyed breath. *Why is he making us learn a whole new way to hit the ball?* she thought. *The old way worked just fine!*

Rose nudged her. "Partners?" she said hopefully.

Andrea nodded. "Sure," she replied.

The two girls moved off to run the drill at the end court, but Andrea couldn't help wondering if Rose thought this new technique was as dumb as she did. Judging by the looks on her teammates' faces, it looked like most of the girls probably did.

Chapter Four

GETTING FRUSTRATED

After school on Monday, Andrea and Rose walked slowly into the rec center. "Is it just me, or is Coach Tucker acting like we've never played volleyball before?" Rose asked.

"I know!" Andrea exclaimed. "I don't know why he's wasting so much time on teaching us how to do basic things like hit the ball. He's not even letting me spend any time on setting! All I'm doing are blocking drills."

Rose sighed. "I wish Coach Warren was still here."

When they arrived at practice, Zoe was already in the gym. She was working on setter footwork on the court by herself. Andrea felt her cheeks flush in annoyance. She should be the one practicing setting!

Another new player named Sophie came out of the locker room and joined Zoe on the court. "Wow, you're getting fast," Sophie said, smiling.

Zoe stopped and pushed an imaginary ball off her forehead. "Coach Tucker gave me some drills to work on at home," she replied. "It's been a lot of work, but I think I'm starting to get the hang of it!"

"Yeah, Coach is great," Sophie agreed. "I'm so glad I made the team this year!"

Andrea frowned. It sounded like the new girls liked Coach Tucker just fine. But they didn't know what they were talking about!

Practice that day was a kamikaze scrimmage, which required four players per court and a lot of position rotations. Andrea tried her best to show Coach Tucker what she could do as a setter, but the only time he seemed to be paying attention to her was when she was blocking — and messing up.

"Blocking is all about good communication and paying attention to the players around you, Andrea," Coach said. She'd just nearly knocked Hannah over while trying to get in front of the ball. "To be successful, a blocker has to read the setter. That means you watch the setter's body position and try to guess where she's going to send the ball."

Andrea blew out a frustrated breath, but she forced herself to nod.

The coach continued: "Try communicating with your teammates so you don't end up running into each other. Let's try again."

Andrea muttered to herself but got back into position. This time the ball came straight toward her, but she moved to block it a second too late. The volleyball hit the floor and bounced to the side of the court.

Coach blew his whistle. "That's enough for today, girls," he said. "Don't forget to practice your solo drills at home. Real games are coming up soon, and we have a lot of new skills to get comfortable with. The more you do them, the faster they'll be there when you need them."

* * *

In the parking lot a few minutes later, Andrea got into her mom's car with a frown and a heavy sigh.

Andrea's mom glanced over at her as she buckled up. "Someone doesn't look very happy. What's the matter, honey?" she asked.

"It's Coach Tucker," Andrea told her. "He's spending so much time on basics and teaching the new girls. He's not even letting me play."

"He's not letting you play?" her mom asked, frowning.

"Well, he is, but he's not letting me play the positions I *know* I'm good at," Andrea explained. "I loved being a setter last year. But now all I'm doing is blocking and running drills on dumb stuff. This isn't fun at all."

Andrea blinked quickly as hot tears began to fill her eyes. She just wanted things to be like they were before.

Her mom was quiet for a minute. "Change is hard sometimes," she said. "You got really good at doing things the old way. It was easy for you. But maybe now you'll learn some new skills and become an even better player."

Andrea sighed and wiped her eyes. "It doesn't feel like it," she said. "It feels like we're going to lose the season because Coach Tucker is messing everything up."

Her mom squeezed her arm. "Your first match is on Friday, right?" she said. "Why don't you give it a few games and see how it goes? Maybe you'll surprise yourself."

Chapter Five

THE FIRST MATCH

That Friday was the Pumas' first match. They were going up against a club named the Golden Eagles, and Andrea was nervous. The Eagles were a strong team. The Pumas had barely beaten them the year before.

How will we manage now? Andrea wondered.

Coach gathered the girls up during their warm-ups. "Okay, ladies," he said. "Here are the positions I want you playing tonight: Sophie, you're on opposite. Rose, outside hitter. Andrea, middle blocker."

Andrea shifted on her feet. Middle blocker? She wasn't too surprised — Coach had her doing lots of blocking drills lately. But she still felt a little disappointed.

Coach Tucker continued reading off his clipboard. "And playing setter . . . Zoe."

Andrea let out a small gasp but quickly covered her mouth. She barely listened as Coach finished going through the positions. Zoe as the setter? But she was so new!

The teams took their places on the court. Andrea tried to focus on the game and not the fact that Zoe was starting their very first match of the season as the setter.

The Eagles had the first serve. The ball flew over the net and headed straight for Emily in the back row. She managed a nice dig, diving to stop the ball before it hit the floor.

Now the volleyball sailed toward Zoe, but she tried to attack it too soon. The ball smashed into the net.

Andrea groaned. *We're doomed!*

The first points all went to the Eagles. The Pumas were making lots of mistakes. First Sophie hit the ball twice in a row, and then Zoe lost control of her set. Andrea's heart sank.

But on the sixth play, they started to turn things around. Zoe set up Rose for a quick kill, and then Andrea managed a couple of solid blocks. As the team began feeling more confident, they began scoring more points. At 20–24, the first set was theirs.

The Pumas were feeling good now. Andrea watched as an Eagles player moved to spike the ball. "I got it!" she yelled.

She leaped up and smacked the ball. It shot back down to the Eagles' side. An Eagles player was caught off guard and hit the ball out of bounds. Point for the Pumas!

Andrea was surprising herself. She was starting to see where an attack might be coming from, and she was calling out to the other blockers to help them get in front of the ball. Maybe all of those drills really were helping. They took the second set by a few points.

"Go, Pumas!" yelled Coach from the side of the court. "Show them what you can do!"

The lead kept going back and forth. The Pumas fell behind and then rallied. But the Eagles pulled ahead and won the third set 25–20. Although Zoe made a few good assists in the fourth set, the Eagles' attacks flew by Andrea. The set went to the Eagles.

The Pumas were having a hard time keeping up now. The team was also making mistakes again. Andrea cringed as Zoe lost a point on a lift, which meant she touched the ball for too long. It was a total rookie mistake.

The set ended quickly with a 15–4 Eagles win. The match was over.

Coach huddled the team together. "You ladies should be very proud," he told them. "I know it wasn't a win, but I saw some wonderful teamwork, and you're all getting out of your comfort zones. Great job, Pumas."

The girls made their way to the locker rooms. Andrea caught up with Rose, who was laughing and chatting with Emily. In fact, Andrea noticed that most of the girls looked pretty excited.

"We definitely have some things to work on," Rose said, "but we did pretty good against the Eagles. And they're such a tough team! Maybe Coach Tucker's strategy isn't so bad."

Andrea gave a small nod. "Yeah, I guess you're right," she admitted. After all, she did feel proud of the blocks she had made, and the team was starting to come together.

But as she sat on a bench to unlace her shoes, Andrea couldn't stop thinking about Zoe's mistakes. If she had been playing setter, there was no doubt in Andrea's mind that the Pumas would have been celebrating a win.

Chapter Six

DIGGING DOUBTS

A few days later at the end of practice, Coach had the girls gather up. "Regional Qualifiers are in October, ladies," he said. "We've had some ups and downs, but with a lot of practice, hard work, and spirit, I think we'll be in great shape for it."

Andrea's stomach filled with butterflies at the mention of Regionals. They had won first place last year, but everything was different now. The coach was rebuilding the team from the ground up.

The Pumas were improving — Andrea felt her own blocking skills getting stronger with every game. But everyone was still settling into new positions. How could they take their game to the next level when players like Zoe were still learning? Andrea wasn't sure.

* * *

The game that night was against a mid-level club called the Tornadoes. Andrea tried to focus as they stepped on the court, but she kept glancing over at Zoe in the setter's position.

Rose made the first serve. The Tornadoes setter quickly got under the ball, her body facing right.

Andrea knew exactly where the ball was going — she was only thinking about volleyball now. "Sophie!" she cried.

Sophie dove right, bouncing the ball off her right arm. The volleyball flew high into the air.

As it came down, Andrea jumped. Her arm came down hard, and the palm of her hand hit the ball with a satisfying *smack*! The ball shot onto the other team's court. Point for the Pumas!

The Pumas were in good shape. Andrea continued to call out plays throughout the match. She loved helping her teammates, and she liked the thrill of stopping an opponent's attack.

Andrea noticed that Zoe was also doing better in her position. She was making fewer mistakes now and was really good at signaling to the Puma attackers where she was going to set the ball.

"Great job, Zoe!" exclaimed Rose after Zoe made a skillful assist. The other girls on the court rushed in for a group hug around her. But Andrea stayed off to the side.

The Tornadoes won the third set, but otherwise the Pumas stayed in control the whole night. It was an easy Puma victory.

* * *

After the game, Andrea was gathering up her things when she felt a hand on her shoulder. It was Coach Tucker.

"Andrea, can I talk to you for a moment?" he asked.

"Oh, sure . . ." she replied. She waved goodbye to Rose, then turned back to Coach.

"You've made some big changes this season," he said. "I just wanted to see how you were feeling about all of it."

Andrea was quiet for a moment. "I wasn't so sure at the start," she admitted. "But the team is getting better with each game, and I know we'll continue to improve. It's just . . ."

"Yes?" Coach asked encouragingly.

"I really liked playing setter last year," Andrea said, sighing. "I don't understand why I got switched to middle blocker."

"Well, during our first practices," said Coach Tucker, "I could tell you had the makings of an excellent blocker. You're one of the tallest girls on the team. With your experience as a setter, you know how a setter thinks. You've had to learn a few new things, but you're already doing such great work."

Andrea smiled. "Thanks," she said, "and I guess lately I have been enjoying blocking."

Coach Tucker smiled back. "I'm glad to hear it," he said. "It takes time and hard work to settle into a position. And Zoe has had to practice her setter skills, too. Maybe you could give her some pointers sometime. I know she would really appreciate it."

Andrea nodded. "I will," she promised. She was about to head for the door, but she had to ask Coach one more thing. "Do you really think we'll be ready for Regionals?"

"If we keep up our hard work, I don't think there's any reason not to be proud of whatever happens, right?" Coach Tucker asked.

Andrea grinned. "Right."

Chapter Seven

EXTRA PRACTICE

On Sunday, with her homework done and volleyball on her mind, Andrea decided to go to the rec center to work on some extra drills. Her mom dropped her off and promised to return in two hours.

As Andrea walked into the center, she could see someone already in the gym. It was Zoe, practicing by herself. Several pieces of brightly colored tape were on the floor. Zoe was using them as targets, setting the ball above the pieces of tape.

Andrea knew that drill — she used to run it all the time as a setter. She felt a small stab of jealousy, but forced it down and walked farther into the gym.

"Hey, Zoe," Andrea said.

Zoe smiled and let the ball bounce to the court floor. "Hi, Andrea!" she called. "Are you getting in some extra practice, too?"

Andrea nodded. "Yep," she said. "Want a partner? I can run some drills with you. Have you tried the eye check yet?"

"No!" Zoe said, looking relieved. "What's that?"

Andrea scooped the ball up from the floor and jogged to the other side of the net. "I'm going to toss the ball to you," she explained. "Set the ball when it comes, but first look at me and yell out if I'm holding up rock, paper, or scissors."

Andrea threw the ball across the net and then jogged a few steps to the side with her fingers raised. Zoe glanced over, a little flustered. "Scissors!" she shouted, getting under the ball and shoving it up into the air.

"Great!" Andrea said.

"What's that one for?" Zoe asked as she tossed the ball back for another try.

"Coach Warren used to run it with me," Andrea explained. "It helps you learn to pay attention to the players, not just the ball. That way you can figure out what they might be planning to do next."

"Cool," Zoe said. "I definitely need to work on that."

The girls ran setting and blocking drills together all morning. Andrea was surprised when she looked up to see her mom standing in the doorway, watching.

"Oops, gotta go," she told Zoe. "Thanks for the practice!"

"No, thank *you*," Zoe said. "That setting drill? Yikes. That was hard, but so helpful!"

"Maybe we can do it again sometime," Andrea said, smiling. Helping Zoe had turned out to be fun — it felt good to share what she knew about setting. And it was nice to get some help on her own skills in return. "Need a ride?"

"That'd be awesome, thanks!" Zoe said.

The girls walked off the court together as Andrea told her friend about going to the National Championships after winning Regionals and how much fun it had been.

Nothing is certain, Andrea thought, *but working as a team, maybe we can get there again.*

Chapter Eight

READY FOR REGIONALS

After two weeks of tough practices, the Pumas were traveling to Regional Qualifiers. They had been working hard and running drills over and over. Now their chances were looking good for the tournament.

On the bus, Andrea still found herself flip-flopping between completely confident and totally freaked out. But most of all, she was excited to see what the new Pumas could do.

The team stepped off the bus and headed to the gym. Inside, the large room was crowded with different volleyball clubs from across the region.

Rose squeezed Andrea's hand tightly. "Ready or not, here we come!" she said, laughing.

Andrea grinned as the team made its way to the locker rooms. The Pumas would play six matches over the two-day event. First up was a match against the Bears, the second-place club from the previous year. Andrea knew it was going to be a difficult start.

Before the match, Coach Tucker motioned for the Pumas to group together on the side of the court. Andrea finished tugging on her knee pads and joined Rose, Zoe, and the rest of her teammates.

"I want you girls to know that you're already winners," Coach said. "No matter what happens, the real prize is playing against better teams, using that experience to strengthen your skills, and giving it your all. Now let's see what you can do. Go, Pumas!"

"PUMAS FOREVER!" they all shouted.

The girls left the huddle and started getting into their positions. But Andrea had to do something first. She jogged over to Zoe.

"Hey, I just wanted to say good luck," Andrea said. "And that I'm glad you decided to join the team. The Pumas are lucky to have a setter as good as you."

A big smile spread across Zoe's face. "Thanks, Andrea!" she replied, blushing a little. "That means a lot." The girls hugged quickly before running to their spots.

Right from the first serve, the Pumas were giving it their all. The gym echoed with the girls yelling and calling out to each other. They were playing like a true team.

But the other team was also playing hard. Their setter was skilled at throwing off the blockers. The Bears took the first and second sets.

By the third set, though, Andrea was reading the setter better and getting ahead of the Bears' attacks. The Pumas pulled together and won the third and fourth sets, forcing a fifth.

But it wasn't enough to save the match. The Bears rallied on the final set and won quickly, 15–7.

"Great effort, ladies. Good communication out there!" Coach said as they jogged off the court.

Andrea wasn't going to let the loss shake her. She was determined to play her best. Zoe, Rose, Emily, and all of her teammates had the same focused look on their faces as they started the second match of the day.

They were up against another middle-ranked club. The Pumas played with the same great teamwork and communication, and this time it paid off. They won the match easily in three sets.

Throughout the rest of the day, the team worked together like never before. Everyone was calling out plays and assisting each other's attacks and blocks. Andrea and Zoe even high-fived after every successful kill.

* * *

That night, the team celebrated the first day of the tournament at a local pizzeria. Andrea was feeling great. The Pumas had lost a total of two games, but they had also won two.

The Pumas' table at the restaurant buzzed with excitement and laughter. And as Andrea bit into her hot slice of pepperoni pizza, she realized she was having more fun playing volleyball with her friends than she had ever had before. She couldn't wait to see what the next day had in store.

Chapter Nine

REMATCH

The Pumas were ready to tackle their last match of the tournament. That morning they had played against another middle-ranked club and had won the game in the fifth set. Andrea and the girls were feeling pumped. Now they were about to face off with a top-ranked club — the Golden Eagles.

I wonder how we'll play against them now, Andrea thought as she took a drink from her water bottle. *So much has changed since our game against them at the start of the season!*

The Golden Eagles jogged confidently onto the court. They'd won five of their matches so far, and the players looked ready to win again.

Andrea gathered her teammates into a huddle. "We can do this, you guys," she said. "We've worked so hard, and we've improved so much. Let's bring it, Pumas!"

The girls cheered. Zoe gave Andrea a smile and a thumbs-up as she got into position.

Emily had the first serve. She tossed the ball into the air, and smacked it over the net. The match had started! The Pumas quickly pulled ahead, 5–0. But the Eagles weren't about to give up. They soon took the lead, 5–8.

Andrea blocked the next hit with a perfect dump right over the net, starting a rally for the Pumas. The two teams stayed within a few points of each other until the end of the set. Finally, the Pumas squeaked out a 25–23 win.

The teams were staying neck-and-neck. Andrea could tell everyone was working their hardest, but the Eagles managed to pull ahead in the second set. First a dump surprised Andrea. Then an attack down the left line flew right past Hannah.

At the end of the third set, Andrea watched as an Eagles player moved to hit the ball. "Hannah, it's coming to you!" she shouted.

Hannah jumped. She sent the ball flying back to Eagles' side. The third set went to the Pumas!

The Pumas kept their focus and continued to score in the fourth set. Zoe perfectly set the ball for Rose, then Rose spiked it. The ball went *thunk!* as it hit the Eagles' court.

The Pumas had won the match! The girls cheered and rushed in for a team hug.

Andrea smiled and laughed as she joined her teammates. They might not be in first place in the tournament overall, but Andrea felt proud. With this win, the Pumas were in third place, and they had really earned it. Coach Tucker's strategy had paid off — the Pumas were learning a lot and having a great time working together as a team!

Chapter Ten

PUMAS FOREVER!

"Over here, girls!" Coach Tucker shouted, herding the team to their seats for the awards ceremony. Everyone was excited. It hadn't been easy, but third place was good enough to send them home with a trophy — and to Nationals.

"Sit here, Andrea!" Emily shouted over the crowd.

"No, here! Sit with me!" Rose said, grabbing her arm.

Zoe plopped into the seat on the other side of her. "You were awesome," she said, bumping her shoulder against Andrea's.

"You were! We all were," Andrea said, bumping her back and grinning.

The officials began the awards ceremony, starting with the team awards. First place went to the Bears and second place to the Golden Eagles. They went up and had their pictures taken with their trophies.

Next up were the third and fourth place teams — the Pumas and the Lionettes! Everyone bunched onto the court with big grins as they held up the trophy.

"Now for the individual awards," an official announced after everyone was seated. The crowd hushed. "Best Offensive Player, with an average of 3.5 kills per set, goes to Tiana Rockwell of the Bears!"

A tall girl in a red uniform jogged onto the court and accepted a trophy from the official. She waved it triumphantly at her team.

"Best Defensive Player, with an average of 5.4 digs per set, goes to Ana Ramos, also of the Bears!" the official continued.

Another girl in a red uniform bounced out onto the court to accept her trophy.

Andrea sighed. Maybe someday the Pumas would be up there getting all these awards!

The official spoke again. "Finally, the All-American Award," he said. "This player was nominated by her coach and teammates for good sportsmanship, leadership, and conduct both on and off the court. From the Pumas . . . Andrea Papin!"

Andrea gasped. Her friends were smiling and shoving her forward before she even knew what was happening. Her eyes filled with surprised tears as she approached the woman holding the trophy.

Andrea took it, waved to the crowd, and ran back to her teammates. "You guys! I can't . . . what?" she said in happy confusion.

"You deserve it, Andrea," Coach Tucker said with a grin. "We made some big changes at the start of the season, but you really rose to the challenge and pulled your teammates up along with you."

Zoe put her arm around Andrea and hugged her tightly. "Pumas forever!" she said.

"PUMAS FOREVER!" everyone shouted together.

Author Bio

Leigh McDonald lives in sunny Tucson, Arizona, with her art teacher husband, two spunky daughters, and two big, crazy dogs. Besides her family and friends, her favorite thing in the world is books — writing, designing, and especially reading them!

Illustrator Bio

Katie Wood fell in love with drawing when she was very small. Since graduating from Loughborough University School of Art and Design in 2004, she has been living her dream working as a freelance illustrator. From her studio in Leicester, England, she creates bright and lively illustrations for books and magazines all over the world.

Glossary

communication (kuh-myoo-ni-KAY-shuhn) — the act of sharing information and ideas

conduct (KON-duhkt) — a person's behavior

drill (DRIL) — a repetitive exercise that helps you learn a specific skill

dig (DIG) — to pass a spiked or fast-moving ball. A player will often dive to reach the ball before it hits the floor.

rally (RAL-lee) — to come back with new energy. In sports, rallying is when a team or player that has been behind starts doing well.

scrimmage (SKRIM-ij) — a practice game

sportsmanship (SPORTS-muhn-ship) — fair play and polite behavior from someone who is competing with others

strategy (STRAT-uh-jee) — a careful plan for accomplishing a specific goal

Discussion Questions

1. Talk about how Andrea felt about Coach Tucker. How did she feel at the start of the season? How did she feel after Regionals? If her feelings were different, what caused the change?

2. Do you think Andrea was right to be upset about not being the setter? Discuss your opinion.

3. Even though the Pumas didn't win first place at Regionals, Andrea and her teammates still felt happy about their performance. Talk about why they felt that way. How would you have felt?

Writing Prompts

1. Which volleyball position would you like to play? Write a paragraph about which position you chose and why.

2. The Pumas did well in Regional Qualifiers, so now they can play in the National Championships. Write a chapter about the Pumas going to Nationals. How do they perform?

3. Zoe worked hard and practiced on her own because she wanted to improve her setter skills. Write 2–3 paragraphs about something that you've worked hard for. How did you practice or prepare? Did you accomplish your goal?

MORE ABOUT VOLLEYBALL POSITIONS

Whether you're a blocker or a setter, every volleyball position plays an important role and can help lead the team to success!

Setter

A setter stays close to the net and sets the ball. She puts the ball up into the air and gets it into a good position for a teammate to spike it. The setter directs the offensive players and makes decisions on who gets the ball and when.

Outside Hitter

An outside hitter covers the front left of the court and is a skilled attacker. She spikes the most throughout the match. The outside hitter also passes and helps block the other team's spikes, so she must be a well-rounded player.

Middle Blocker

A middle blocker tries to keep the other team from getting the ball over the net. She's often the tallest player on the team. The middle blocker directs the other front row players and helps plan the team's blocking strategy.

Opposite

An opposite covers the front right side of the court and both blocks and hits. The position gets its name because the player always plays opposite of the setter. If the setter can't get to the ball, the opposite will set it.

Libero

A libero is a skilled defensive player who only plays in the back row. She wears a different colored jersey, because special rules apply to her. The libero makes a lot of passes and digs to help keep the ball in play.

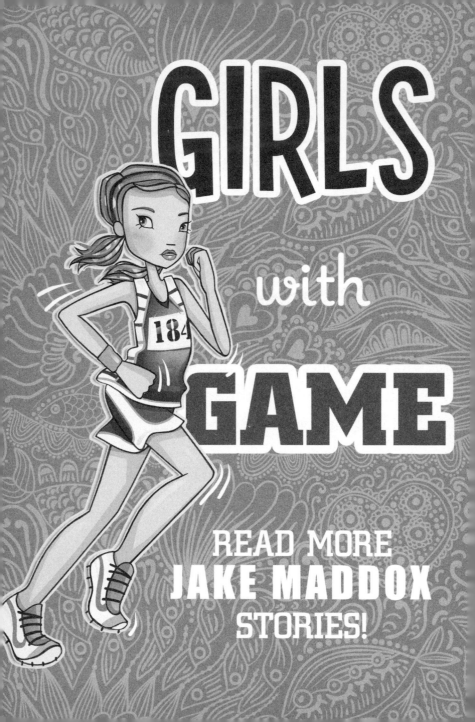

GIRLS

with

GAME

READ MORE
JAKE MADDOX
STORIES!